MONSTER HEROES

WITCH'S BREW

BY BLAKE HOENA
ILLUSTRATED BY DAVE BARDIN

Raintree is an imprint of Capstone Global Library Limited, a company incorporated in England and Wales having its registered office at 264 Banbury Road, Oxford, OX2 7DY – Registered company number: 6695582

www.raintree.co.uk
myorders@raintree.co.uk
Text © Capstone Global Library Limited 2017
The moral rights of the proprietor have been asserted.

Edited by Christianne Jones
Designed by Ted Williams
Original illustrations © 2017
Illustrated by Dave Bardin
Production by Katy LaVigne
Originated by Capstone Press
Printed and bound in China

ISBN 978 1 4747 2783 9
20 19 18 17 16
10 9 8 7 6 5 4 3 2 1

British Library Cataloguing in Publication Data
A full catalogue record for this book is available from
the British Library.

Photo credits: Shutterstock: kasha_malasha, design element, popular business, design element

CONTENTS

MINA (the Vampire)

Mina thinks people taste like dirty socks, so beet juice is her snack of choice. Its red color has fooled her parents into thinking that she's a traditional blood-sucking vampire instead of a superhero hopeful. She has the ability to change into a bat or a mouse at will.

Brian is the brainy one amongst his friends. Unlike other zombies, Brian prefers tofu to brains. No matter what sort of trouble is brewing, Brian always comes up with a plan to save the day, like a true superhero.

BRIAN (the Zombie)

WILL (the Ghost)

Will is quite shy. Luckily he can turn invisible any time he wants because he is a ghost. When Will is doing good deeds, he likes to remain unseen. His invisibility helps him act brave like a real superhero.

With a wave of her wand and a poetic chant, Linda can reverse any magical curse. She hopes to use her magic to help people, just like a superhero would.

LINDA (the Witch)

A FAMILIAR PROBLEM

"*Peep! Peep!*"

"What is it, Petey?" Linda asked her pet caterpillar.

All witches had a familiar. This special pet helped them do witchy stuff. Witches understood their familiars even though they didn't talk.

Petey peeped again.

"Oh, no!" Linda gasped. "Griselda and Agnes are using Mum's cauldron!"

"*Squeak*!" Petey squealed. That meant yes.

Linda ran to the kitchen and peeked in. Her sisters and their familiars circled a large, black cauldron. Griselda had a black cat named Scratch. Agnes had a snake named Slither.

"They must be brewing a potion," Linda whispered to Petey.

"Eye of newt and toe of frog," Griselda cackled.

"Wool of bat and tongue of dog," Agnes screeched.

"Double, double toil and trouble," Griselda chanted.

"Fire burn and cauldron bubble," Agnes sang.

Agnes threw something into the pot. *Bam*!

"Eek!" Linda squealed in fear.

Her sisters turned to Linda.

"What are YOU doing here?" Griselda asked.

"Go away! You'll ruin our potion — again," Agnes said.

Griselda stepped in front of the pot as Agnes pushed Linda out of the room.

"But I —" Linda tried to say.

Bang! The kitchen door slammed shut.

Linda ran back to her room. She knew her sisters were up to no good. She called her friends.

Linda's friends were not like other monsters. They did not scare people. They wanted to help people and save the day, like superheroes.

"Meet me at our secret hideout," she told her friends.

CHAPTER 2

SUPER FRIENDS

Linda and Petey rushed to the cemetery. They found the tall oak tree and quickly climbed up. Then they crawled through a trap door leading into their hideout.

Inside, Mina and Will were waiting. Linda did not see Brian. Zombies were always late.

As they waited for Brian, Linda
told her friends about her sisters'
new potion.

"What does it do?" Mina asked.

Linda shrugged. "I don't know."

"I bet it's something horrible," Will said.

"I *know* it's something horrible," Linda said.

"That's why we can't let them use their potion," Brian said as he climbed up the ladder into the hideout.

Everyone agreed.

"We need to know their plan," Brian said.

"But they won't let me near the potion," Linda said.

"I can spy on them," Mina said. *Poof!* Mina turned into a bat.

"Awesome," Brian said.

"I'll be right back," Mina the bat squeaked. She fluttered out the window and flew away.

The others waited and waited and waited. When Mina the bat returned, she changed back into her vampire form. *Poof!*

"Awesome," Brian said again.

"What are they doing?" Linda asked.

"They are setting up a lemonade stand," Mina explained.

"*Peep! Peep!*" Petey squeaked.

"I know, Petey," Linda said. "They didn't use any lemons in their potion. Not one."

THAT'S NOT LEMONADE

Griselda and Agnes were in the front yard. They sat at a table with the bubbling cauldron. Linda and her friends hid behind a bush.

"Listen up! I have a plan," Linda said. "But first, I need a real lemon."

"Where are we going to find one of those?" Brian asked.

Mina dug into her pocket. She
pulled out a bright yellow lemon.

"Why did you have a lemon in
your pocket?" Brian asked.

"I like sucking on them," Mina
said with a smile.

Following Linda's plan, Brian walked over to the lemonade stand.

"Hmmm," he said. "I don't know what to order."

"All we have is lemonade," Agnes said.

"Yeah, just lemonade," Griselda said.

Mina changed into a mouse. She ran across the pavement to keep people away.

Will had taken off his sheet. He was now invisible. He carried the lemon to the cauldron and dropped it into the pot.

Linda quietly chanted, "Lemon! Lemon! Yellow and bright. Give my sisters a nasty fright."

Bam!

"What happened?" Agnes coughed.

"I don't know," Griselda said.

"Um, I don't think I'm thirsty anymore," Brian said as he quickly ran off.

Mina turned back into a vampire. All of the friends hid behind the bush again. They watched as smoke spread out from the witch's brew.

"I think something's wrong," Griselda said to Agnes.

"You think?" Agnes said, annoyed.

Critters were gathering all around the sisters. Mice scurried along the ground. Squirrels scampered through the trees.

"Those critters look really hungry," Agnes said.

"The potion was supposed to turn people into animals so we could roast them for supper," Griselda shrieked.

"Not make animals want to turn *us* into dinner," Agnes cried.

The sisters screamed and ran away. The animals chased after them at full speed.

Linda and her friends laughed.

"We saved the day," Will said.

"We make a great team," Linda said.

Everyone agreed.

DAVE BARDIN

Dave Bardin studied illustration at Cal State Fullerton while working as an art teacher. As an artist, Dave has worked on many different projects for television, books, comics and animation. In his spare time Dave enjoys watching documentaries, listening to podcasts, traveling and spending time with friends and family. He works out of Los Angeles, CA, USA.

BLAKE A. HOENA

Blake A. Hoena grew up in central Wisconsin, USA, where he wrote stories about robots conquering the moon and trolls lumbering around the woods behind his parents house. He now lives in Minnesota, USA, and continues to write about fun things like space aliens and superheroes. Blake has written more than fifty chapter books and graphic novels for children.

WITCH'S GLOSSARY

brew make something, such as coffee, tea, or a potion

cauldron large, black pot used to brew potions

cemetery place where dead people are buried; also, a good place for a monster hideout

chant to say words in a rhythmic way, like when casting a spell

familiar witch's pet, such as a cat or snake

hideout secret place

ingredient one part of a recipe to make food or potions

invisible impossible to see

potion magical drink

THINK ABOUT IT

1. Linda and her sisters have very different names for their familiars. Why do you think that is? How do each of the names fit their familiars?

2. In this story, each of the characters play a part in the plan to stop Linda's sisters. Who do you feel played the most important part and why? Who played the least important part and why?

3. Linda's sisters use their magic to do bad things. What could Linda do to make them change their ways?

WRITE ABOUT IT

1. If you could have a familiar, what would it be? Write a paragraph describing your familiar and why you picked it.

2. Linda and her sisters create chants to cast spells. Write down a spell of your own. What does your spell do?

3. Pretend you are Linda and write a journal entry about your evil sisters.